RABBIT & BEAR

A Bite in the Night

STORY BY
JULIAN GOUGH

ILLUSTRATIONS BY
JIM FIELD

HODDER

For my good friend Tony who I've known since the age of 5.
The best drawer and Lego maker.

J.F.

●

Perhaps the luckiest thing that ever happened to me was
having a great dad (because not everyone gets a good one).
So this book is dedicated to my father, Richard Gough. He
didn't have much of a dad himself, and so he had to work out
how to do it all from scratch. He did an amazing job.
(And in his spare time, he fought a lot of fires, and saved
a lot of lives.) I love you, Dad. Thanks for everything.

J.G.

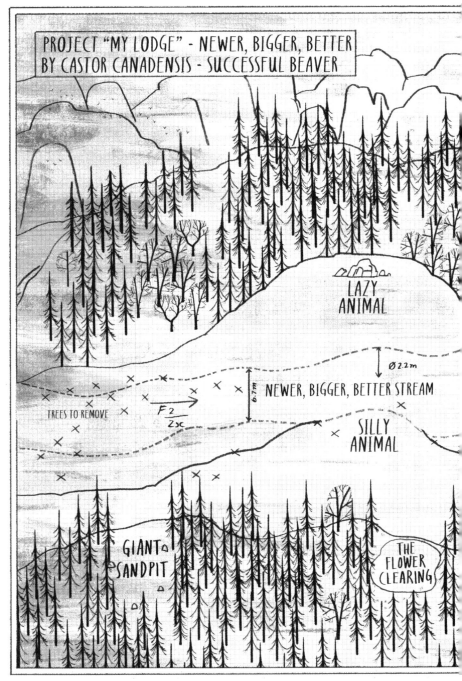

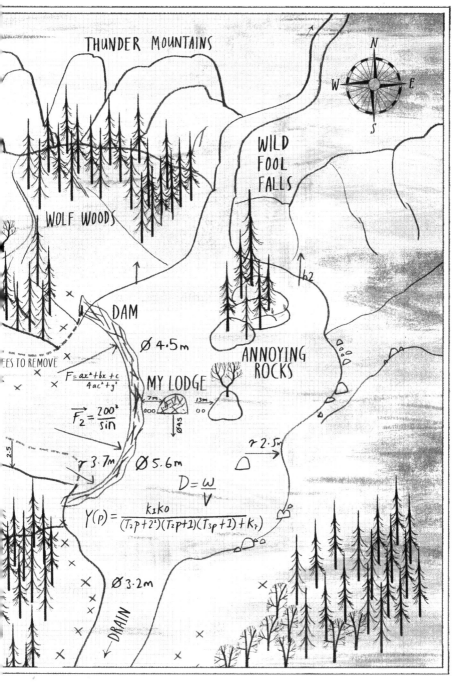

Rabbit burst into Bear's cave.

"Bear, where do trees go for the Winter?" said Rabbit.

"Trees stay exactly where they are," said Bear, yawning. "You're thinking of birds. Birds fly south for the Winter."

"Well, I think some trees are flying south this year, Bear."

"But trees can't fly," said Bear, "… I think." She tried to reach an early-morning itch, right in the middle of her back. "Ooof … Can you scratch my itch? It's just there."

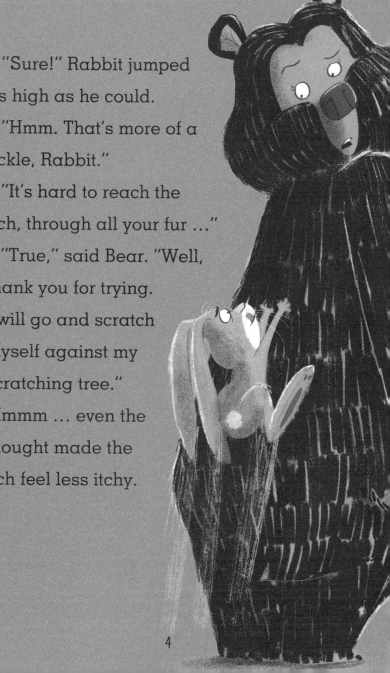

"Sure!" Rabbit jumped
as high as he could.

"Hmm. That's more of a
tickle, Rabbit."

"It's hard to reach the
itch, through all your fur ..."

"True," said Bear. "Well,
thank you for trying.
I will go and scratch
myself against my
scratching tree."
Mmmm ... even the
thought made the
itch feel less itchy.

"Er, Bear ..." said Rabbit.

But Bear was already walking down to the stream. She looked left. She looked right. "Where—" said Bear.

"That's what I'm trying to tell you …" said Rabbit, catching up.

"Where is my favourite scratching tree?"

"Flying south, for the Winter?" said Rabbit.

Bear looked up into the sky, just in case.

"No …"

Then Rabbit saw something. He gulped, and pointed down.

Bear looked.

There, where her scratching tree had been, was a *stump*. Bear bent closer. A stump covered in *tooth marks*.

Giant tooth marks.

Rabbit's knees began to tremble. "Wh … wh … what kind of ferocious Monster could EAT a TREE?"

"I don't know," said Bear. "A hungry one? Which reminds me, let's get some honey, to put on berries, for breakfast."

"WHY AREN'T YOU WORRYING?" shouted Rabbit.

"Because worrying doesn't fix things,"
said Bear. "But breakfast does."

So Bear and Rabbit went to look for the
Honey Bee Tree.

But the Honey Bee
Tree was gone.
The stump was
covered with giant
tooth marks.
"Are you worried
yet?" said Rabbit.

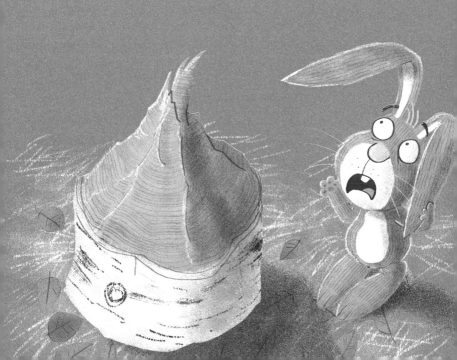

"Hmmm," said Bear.
"Woodpecker lives in a tree …"
"Oh *no*," said Rabbit.
Rabbit ran, and Bear
walked, until they could
see Woodpecker's tree.
"Oh, it's still there!"
said Rabbit. His knees
and elbows stopped
trembling. "Hi,
Woodpecker!"

"Hi! Hi! Hi!" shouted Woodpecker from her nest. "I'll be out in a minute! I'm packing! To Go! Go! Go!"

"Where?" said Bear.

"South! For the Winter! More Parties! More Fun! Fun! Fun! Warmer! HA HA HA!"

"I'll miss you, Woodpecker," said Rabbit. "And your drumming." Rabbit sighed. No more music and dancing in the long evenings …

Then a loud CRUNCH! came from Very Near By.

It sounded like the world's largest rabbit, eating the world's largest carrot.

CRUNCH!

Like a Monster Rabbit, thought Rabbit … eating a Monster Carrot … to give it the energy … to Attack!

This time Rabbit trembled so much, he was worried his ears would fall off.

CRUNCH!

"It's coming from behind that bush!" said Rabbit.

Woodpecker's tree trembled.

"Hey, hey, hey, Bear!" shouted Woodpecker. "Stop shaking my tree!"

"I'm not shaking your tree," said Bear, puzzled.

"Then who is?" said Woodpecker. She stuck her head out to look.

Another CRUNCH! came from behind the bush. The loudest CRUNCH! yet.

Woodpecker's tree
began to fall.
"Help! Help!"
shouted Woodpecker.
"The world is falling
over sideways!
Someone catch the
world!"
Bash! Crash!

Smash! SPLASH!

The top of the tree landed in the water.

So did Woodpecker.

"Hurgle! Gurgle!" said Woodpecker, with
her tail trapped under the tree. "Wurgle!
Murgle! SPLURGLE!"

Bear stepped into the water and pulled
Woodpecker free. But … Pop! Pop! Pop!
"Owwa! Owwa! Owwa!"
"Oh no," said Rabbit.
"Your tail feathers!"
Woodpecker stared
at her bare bum.
"Gone!"

"Can you still fly?" said Bear.

"I'll try!" She tried to fly in a
straight line. "Great! I'm flying
south! … No, west! … No, north! … No,
east! Wwwoooooooooaaaaaaahhhh!"

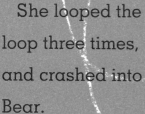

She looped the
loop three times,
and crashed into
Bear.

"OOOF," said
Bear. "Oh dear.
Well, your tail
will grow back
by Spring."

"But but but Spring comes after Winter!" said Woodpecker. "That's too late! I'll freeze!"

"Can you make a new nest," said Rabbit, "at the top of a new tree?"

"I can't fly that high, with no tail!"

"Oh dear," said Bear. "So where are you going to live for the Winter?"

"I don't know!" said Woodpecker. "My house is underwater. I don't want to live underwater! Fish pee there!"

"Wait …" said Bear,
and turned to Rabbit.
"You didn't live right
beside the stream
yesterday …"

"No," said Rabbit, "no, I didn't."
"Why did you move your
burrow?" said Woodpecker
fiercely to Rabbit.

"I didn't move my burrow!" said Rabbit. "Someone moved the stream!"

The water rose even further, and
Woodpecker's house floated away.

"I am very close to being slightly worried,"
said Bear.

"Slightly worried?" said Rabbit. "SLIGHTLY WORRIED?! The stream is climbing the hill! All the trees are falling over! IT'S THE END OF THE WORLD!"

"Oh," said Bear, "I don't think it's that bad."

"Yes yes yes it is!" said Woodpecker. "My house just floated around the bend. I'm going to freeze into an icicle. An icicle with an extra-cold bum!"

"Ah well," said Rabbit, relaxing at last. "At least things absolutely, definitely can't possibly get any worse …"

The bush shook. What was
in the bush? Oh no, he'd
forgotten …

"AAAAaaah!" shouted
Rabbit. "The Monster!"

The Monster came out from behind the bush.

"Aaaargh!" said Rabbit. "The Monster's teeth are enormous!"

"Er, yes," said Bear. "True. But the actual Monster is … quite small."

The Monster walked up to them, reading
a piece of bark. It had the biggest two front
teeth they had ever seen.

The Monster bumped into Bear's knee.
It looked up.

"Move, silly animal," said the Monster.
"You are standing in the way of
Progress."

"What's Progress?" said Bear.

"Progress is making things ... Newer!"

CRUNCH!

"Bigger!"

CRUNCH!

"Better!"

CRUNCH!

And the creature chewed through a small tree like it was a carrot. Rabbit jumped out of the way as it fell.

"You think this is making things Better?" said Rabbit. "You Monster!"

"I'm not a Monster," said the creature. "Monsters don't exist. Only very silly animals believe in Monsters."

"OK, OK, OK, if you're not a Monster," said Woodpecker, "then WHAT WHAT WHAT are you?"

"You can call me … *Castor Canadensis*,"
said the creature.

"Eh?" said Rabbit.

"It is the scientific name for the North
American Beaver," said Castor Canadensis.

"Why did you move our stream, Castor?" said Woodpecker.

"I didn't move it," said Castor. "I'm just making it Bigger. And therefore Better. Progress!"

"But ..." said Bear, "how do you make a stream bigger?"

"Engineering!" said Castor.

"You put an Engine in our stream?!" said Rabbit.

"No, silly rabbit!" said Castor. "Engineering is the Science of Building Newer, Bigger, Better things." He waved at the deeper, wider stream. "Progress!"

"What has that got to do with our missing trees?" said Bear.

"Everything! Follow me, silly animals, and I'll show you."

They followed Castor around the bend.
Just where their stream normally flowed
into the lake, it was blocked, by a dam
made of trees. Very familiar trees …

"My scratching tree!" said Bear.

"Our honey tree!" said Rabbit.

"My home!" said Woodpecker.

"Well, it's New," said Bear, looking at the dam. "And Big. But I'm not sure if it's Better. What will it do?"

"Oh, nothing much," said Castor. "Just flood your valley."

"Flood?" said Rabbit.

"Flood?!" said
Woodpecker.
"How deep?"
said Bear.
"Oh," said
Castor, "not very
deep." He raised
his hand to slightly
above Rabbit's head.

"Just this high."

Rabbit looked up, horrified. "The stream will come in my back door! AND OVER MY HEAD!"

"Yes," said Castor. "If I do it right."

CRUNCH! CRUNCH! CRUNCH!

CRASH …

"Well, animals can move house," said Bear. "But what happens to the trees in the valley? Their roots will be underwater."

"Oh, all those trees there will rot," said Castor, stopping work for a moment to point.

"That's terrible!" said Rabbit.

"That's great!" said Bear.

"That's the best best best thing ever!" said Woodpecker. "OK, build your dam!"

"WHAT?" said Rabbit.

"Rotten trees are much much much easier to peck holes in," said Woodpecker. "And rotten trees have lots and LOTS more beetles …"

"... and beetles' eggs," said Bear, "and honey bee nests and ..." It was all too yummy for Bear.

"Ugh!" said Rabbit.
"You dribbled on my
head!"

"Sorry," said Bear.

The water rose higher, and began to drip through Rabbit's back door.

"Castor!" said Rabbit. "This is a disaster!"

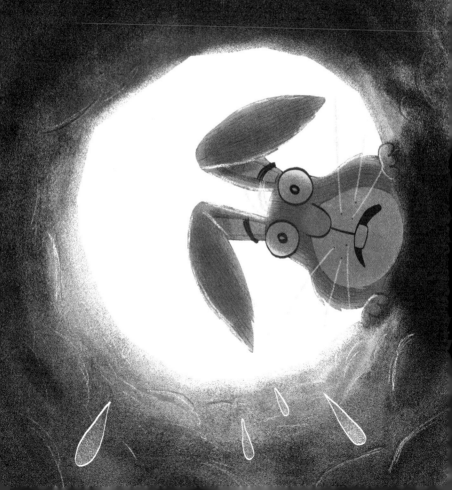

"Don't worry," said Castor. "I've done an Important Official Scientific Report. It's full of Good News." He handed the piece of bark to Rabbit. "See?"

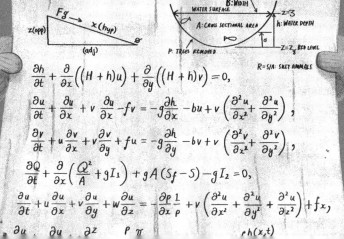

ENVIRONMENTAL IMPACT REPORT FOR HYDRO-ENGINEERING PROJECT

BY CASTOR CANADENSIS (SUCCESSFUL BEAVER)

THE SCIENTIFIC FORMULA FOR
WATER FLOWING IN A STREAM PAST SOME SILLY ANIMALS IS:

Fg → x (hyp)

z(opp)

(adj)

B: WIDTH

WATER SURFACE

$z = 3$

A: CROSS SECTIONAL AREA

h: WATER DEPTH

P: TREES REMOVED

$Z = Z_s$ BED LEVEL

$R = S/A$: SILLY ANIMALS

$$\frac{\partial h}{\partial t} + \frac{\partial}{\partial x}\left((H + h)u\right) + \frac{\partial}{\partial y}\left((H + h)v\right) = 0,$$

$$\frac{\partial u}{\partial t} + \frac{\partial u}{\partial x} + v\frac{\partial u}{\partial x} - fv = -g\frac{\partial h}{\partial x} - bu + v\left(\frac{\partial^2 u}{\partial x^2} + \frac{\partial^2 u}{\partial y^2}\right),$$

$$\frac{\partial v}{\partial t} + u\frac{\partial v}{\partial x} + v\frac{\partial v}{\partial y} + fu = -g\frac{\partial h}{\partial y} - bv + v\left(\frac{\partial^2 v}{\partial x^2} + \frac{\partial^2 v}{\partial y^2}\right),$$

$$\frac{\partial Q}{\partial t} + \frac{\partial}{\partial x}\left(\frac{Q^2}{A} + gI_1\right) + gA(S_f - S) - gI_2 = 0,$$

$$\frac{\partial u}{\partial t} + u\frac{\partial u}{\partial x} + v\frac{\partial u}{\partial y} + w\frac{\partial u}{\partial z} = -\frac{\partial p}{\partial x}\frac{1}{\rho} + v\left(\frac{\partial^2 u}{\partial x^2} + \frac{\partial^2 u}{\partial y^2} + \frac{\partial^2 u}{\partial z^2}\right) + f_x,$$

"See what?"
Rabbit stared
at it upside down.

He stared at it sideways.

He put it the right way round
and stood on his own head.
No, it was far too Official and
Scientific for him to understand.
"Tell me in Small, Simple
Words," said Rabbit.

"Sure," said Castor. He looked at the report over Rabbit's shoulder, and turned it back into Small, Simple Words. "A dam will be good news for beavers, fish, snakes, honeybees, tortoises, blue jays, beetles, wolves, frogs, bears, and woodpeckers."

"Huh," said Rabbit. "It can't be good news for EVERYONE."

"No," said Castor. "It's bad news for ... let me see." He turned the page. "Oh yes ..."

BAD NEWS FOR

RABBITS

"AaaAAaaAAaargh!" said Rabbit. "And who else is it bad news for?"

"Oh, just rabbits," said Castor. "But rabbits are usually not very popular, because of their Bad Habits. So the other animals don't mind at all."

Then Mole and Mouse and Vole arrived.

"Hey!" said Mole in his squeaky voice.
"You've flooded my house! I'm angry!"

"Hey!" said Mouse, in her even squeakier
voice. "You've flooded *my* house! I'm
furious!"

"Hey!" squeaked Vole, the youngest and
smallest of all, in a voice so squeaky they
could hardly hear it. She was so angry she

climbed all the way up Castor's fur, to shout in his ear. "You've flooded MY house! And that's MEAN!"

"Oh yes," said Castor, and brushed Vole off his shoulder like she was an annoying leaf. "I forgot." He scribbled on his report. "It's also bad news for moles, and mice, and voles. But they are Small and Unimportant and Silly Animals. Well, I'd better get back to work."

CRUNCH! CRUNCH! CRUNCH!

CRASH ...

"What kind of Monster are you?!" shouted Rabbit.

"Stop calling me a Monster!" said Castor. "I'm a beaver, and beavers are Very Important and Successful Animals."

"Yeah, successful at *ruining people's lives*," said Rabbit.
"I don't think he *means* to ruin our lives," said Bear.

Rabbit turned to face Bear
and Woodpecker. "You would
say that! You're Monsters, too!"
"Us?" said Bear, shocked.
"Why?"
"Because you're going to
help him flood my home, just to
get more honey and delicious
beetles' eggs."

"Yes, yes, yes," said Woodpecker, with a sigh. "I guess guess guess we are. But, you know … Delicious beetles' eggs! YUM! YUM! YUM!"

"No," said Bear. "We're not. We are going to help you, Rabbit."

CRUNCH! CRUNCH! ...

"WHAT?" said Castor. He was so surprised, he stopped chewing.

"Help me?" said Rabbit, stunned.

"Listen," said Castor, "if you help that silly rabbit, you won't get all of my lovely delicious rotten trees. And only a STUPID animal would throw away all those tasty beetles' eggs and honey."

Bear shrugged.
"Rabbit is my friend."
"OK, OK, OK," said
Woodpecker. "We'll
both help Rabbit.
He's my friend too."

73

"But … That's Illogical! Irrational! INCOMPREHENSIBLE!" said Castor.

"Say it in Smaller, Simpler Words!" said Rabbit.

"It doesn't make sense!" said Castor.

"Oh," said Rabbit, and then said, "Oooof …" as Bear and Woodpecker hugged him, and he hugged them back.

"What's happening to your face?" said Castor.

"I'm smiling," said Rabbit.

"What's ... *that*?" asked Castor.

"It's when you're so full to the top with happiness, it floods out."

"Really?" said Castor. "*My* face has never done that."

"You've never smiled?"
said Bear. "Then how
can you possibly be
successful?"

"I am a Success, because … because beavers work harder than any other animal!" said Castor. "We cut down trees all day, WITH JUST OUR TEETH. Build dams! Build lodges! It's incredibly hard work, and totally exhausting."

"Uh-huh," said Bear. "And what is the Point?"

Castor looked all around him, and up, and down. "The Point of what?" he said cautiously.

"The Point of all this work," said Bear.

"Well … I work incredibly hard all week, so I can stop work at the weekend."

"OK," said Woodpecker. "So what do you do do do at the weekend?"

"Just … sort of … sit."

"With all your friends?" said Bear.

"What are friends?" said Castor.

"Other animals that you like," said Bear.

"And who like you," said Rabbit.

"And that you play with," said
Woodpecker.

"… and talk with," said Mole, "… and
laugh with," said Mouse, "… and dance
with," squeaked Vole, who liked dancing.

"Oh, I don't have any time for that
nonsense," said Castor.
"*Dance?* By the weekend,
I'm too tired to *move*."

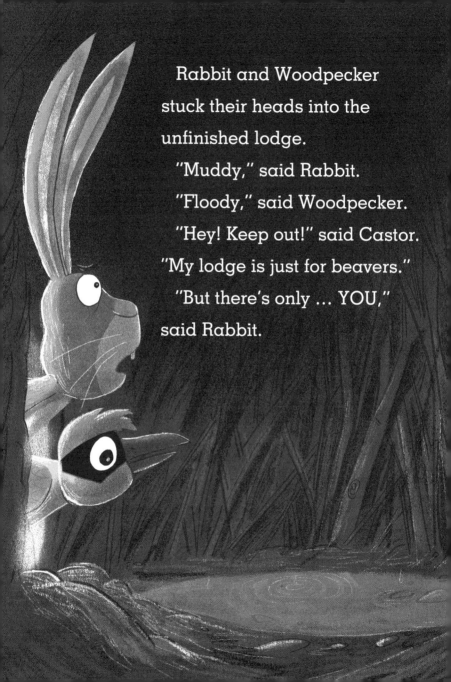

Rabbit and Woodpecker stuck their heads into the unfinished lodge.

"Muddy," said Rabbit.

"Floody," said Woodpecker.

"Hey! Keep out!" said Castor. "My lodge is just for beavers."

"But there's only ... YOU," said Rabbit.

"Well ... yes," said Castor.

"So you work too hard, and you're always tired, and you have no friends," said Bear. "And you sit in the dark, alone, in a muddy, floody hole, all Winter ..." She put an arm around Castor's shoulder. "Poor Castor."

"Stop!" said Castor, putting his paws over his ears. "You're making it sound like I'm not Successful!"

"But you aren't successful," said Rabbit. "Everybody hates you. Your life's a disaster."

"I never thought of it like that before," said Castor. He sat down and started to cry.

Bear frowned at Rabbit. Rabbit shrugged.

Bear said to Castor, "Look, what if we all help you?"

"Help me?"

"Yes, help you to build your lodge."

"But not just for beavers," said Rabbit. "And not so muddy. And floody."

"Bigger?" said Castor. "And better?"

"Yes! We'll build a Club!" said Bear. "For all the animals that don't sleep through the Winter, like Rabbit, or can't fly away, like Woodpecker."

"And we could dance, in the evenings …" said Rabbit.

"And sleep there, all together, at night …" said Woodpecker. "Warm! Warm! Warm!"

"Sleepovers!" said Mole and Mouse and Vole, and they hugged each other so hard that all three of them farted.

"You mean … you want to be my …"

"Friends!" shouted all the animals, so loud that Owl woke up and joined them.

Castor looked at all their smiling faces. "OK," he said. "I'll try it."

"Good!" said Bear. "OK, first of all, Rabbit needs to move above the flood."

Bear and Owl and Castor and Mole all helped Rabbit dig a new back door, higher up the hill.

"I think I'm starting to understand friendship!" said Castor.

He was so excited,
he cut down a
REALLY big tree with
his amazing teeth.

CRUNCH!
CRUNCH!
CRUNCH!
CRASH ...

Castor tried to roll it into the stream, but it was too heavy.

"Let me help," said Bear. She pushed too, and the tree rolled.

Splash!

"Ah, that's how helping works!" said Castor. "When a friend helps, it weighs half as much! So it's twice as easy! Mathematics!"

And together, using the special
mathematics of friendship, all the animals
built the dam. Then they built the lodge.
Then they slapped mud on the walls. Then
they slapped mud on each other, and had a
lovely messy time.

Inside, the little animals wove a springy, bouncy dance floor out of sticks and twigs. BOING! BOING! BOING!

Even little Vole made beds of crisp dry leaves, for sleeping.

Castor crossed out "MY LODGE" and wrote "OUR CLUB" in neat letters on bark.

They all looked around their brand new Happy Dancing Club and Sleepover Palace.

"It's New!" said Castor.

"And it's Better!" said Rabbit.

"It's … Progress!" said Woodpecker. "Wow! Wow! Wow! Wow! Wow! Wow! Wow!"

"Zzzz …" snored Bear. "Hm? Oh! Time for me to go to sleep for the Winter, I think. So will you all be OK?"

"Sure!" said Rabbit, and Woodpecker, and Castor, and Owl, and Mole, and Mouse, and Vole. "See you in Spring!"

And Bear went back to her cave to sleep, and had the best dreams ever. ZzzzZZzzzZzzzz …

And all the other animals went into their Dancing Club, and played music and drummed and laughed and danced.

All except Castor, who just stood back and watched.

"Want to dance?" said Rabbit to Castor.

"Thank you," said Castor shyly. "But I don't know how."

"I'll show you," said Rabbit.

And Rabbit showed Castor how to dance.

Castor looked around at all his
new friends dancing. His face
creaked, and began to move.

"Something funny is happening
to your face," said Rabbit,
alarmed. "Are you OK?
How do you feel?"

"I feel very, very Successful," Castor said,
and he smiled an enormous smile.

JULIAN GOUGH

© Andreas Riemenschneider 2015

Julian Gough is an award-winning novelist, playwright, poet, musician and scriptwriter.
He was born in London, grew up in Ireland and now lives in Berlin.

Among many other things, Julian wrote the ending to **Minecraft**, the world's most successful computer game for children of all ages.

He likes to drink coffee and steal pigs.

Jim Field is an award-winning illustrator, character designer and animation director.
He grew up in Farnborough, worked in London and now lives in Paris.

His first picture book, **Cats Ahoy!**, written by Peter Bently, won the Booktrust Roald Dahl Funny Prize. He is perhaps best known for drawing frogs on logs in the bestselling **Oi Frog**.

He likes playing the guitar and drinking coffee.

JIM FIELD

© Sandy Fouchérand 2016

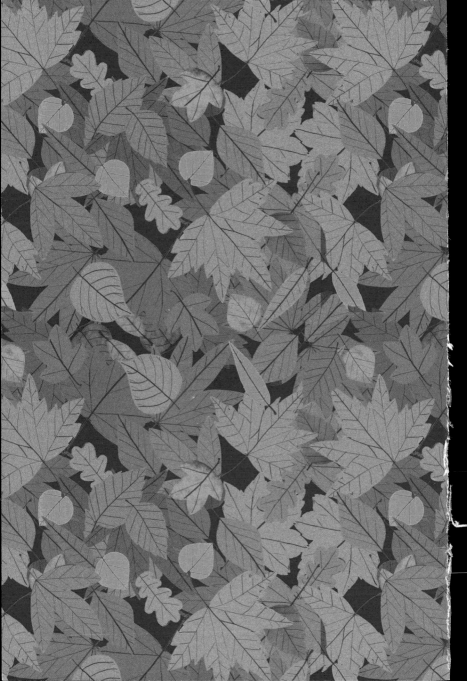